Lerner SPORTS

SPORTS' GREATEST OF ALL TIME

TENNIS'S G.O.A.T.

SERENA WILLIAMS, ROGER FEDERER, AND MORE

JON M. FISHMAN

Lerner Publications ◆ Minneapolis

Copyright © 2022 by Lerner Publishing Group, Inc.

Lerner Publications Company
An imprint of Lerner Publishing Group, Inc.
241 First Avenue North
Minneapolis, MN 55401 USA

For reading levels and more information, look up this title at www.lernerbooks.com.

Main body text set in Aptifer Sans LT Pro.Typeface provided by Linotype AG.

Editor: Brianna Kaiser **Designer:** Kim Morales **Photo Editor:** Brianna Kaiser

Library of Congress Cataloging-in-Publication Data

Names: Fishman, Jon M., author.
Title: Tennis's G.O.A.T. : Serena Williams, Roger Federer, and more / Jon M. Fishman.
Other titles: Tennis's greatest of all time
Description: Minneapolis : Lerner Publications, [2022] | Series: Sports' greatest of all time (Lerner sports) | Includes bibliographical references and index. | Audience: Ages 7–11 | Audience: Grades 2–3 | Summary: "Grab your racket, head to the courts, and ace that serve! It's time to learn about the greatest tennis players of all time. Readers will be presented with exciting stats in a fun top-10 format"—Provided by publisher.
Identifiers: LCCN 2020054215 (print) | LCCN 2020054216 (ebook) | ISBN 9781728428642 (library binding) | ISBN 9781728431604 (paperback) | ISBN 9781728430843 (ebook)
Subjects: LCSH: Tennis players—Juvenile literature. | Tennis—Juvenile literature.
Classification: LCC GV996.5 .F57 2022 (print) | LCC GV996.5 (ebook) | DDC 796.342092/2 [B]—dc23

LC record available at https://lccn.loc.gov/2020054215
LC ebook record available at https://lccn.loc.gov/2020054216

Manufactured in the United States of America
1-49401-49502-3/12/2021

TABLE OF CONTENTS

In 1938, Don Budge won all four majors and became the sport's first Grand Slam winner.

FIRST SERVE

Sports fans love to think about star athletes and rank the greatest of all time (G.O.A.T.). But in tennis, ranking the all-time best players is tough. People have played modern tennis for about 150 years. But the sport's origins go back much further than that.

FACTS AT A GLANCE

BJÖRN BORG won Wimbledon five years in a row.

CHRIS EVERT won more than 90 percent of her pro matches.

In 2020, **RAFAEL NADAL** tied Roger Federer with 20 wins at major events.

SERENA WILLIAMS holds the modern record with 23 major tournament wins.

In 11th-century France, people played *jeu de paume*. Using just their hands, players hit a ball against a wall or over a rope. Later, athletes began to use thick, webbed gloves or wooden paddles to hit the ball. In the 16th century, rackets replaced gloves and paddles.

In 1874, a British military officer wrote a book of rules that became the basis for modern tennis. The sport was part of the Summer Olympics from 1896 to 1924.

By the 1930s, four major tournaments had become the sport's most important events. They included the Australian Open, the French Open, the US Open, and Wimbledon. In 1938, Don Budge won all four majors. He became the first player to secure the Grand Slam. Tennis returned to the Olympics in 1988.

Tennis court surfaces vary depending on the event. Most are grass, clay, or hard-court surfaces. Wimbledon is a grass-surface event, and the French Open is played on clay. The US Open and Australian Open are hard-court events.

People have played modern tennis for over 100 years. Here, fans watch a tennis match in 1922.

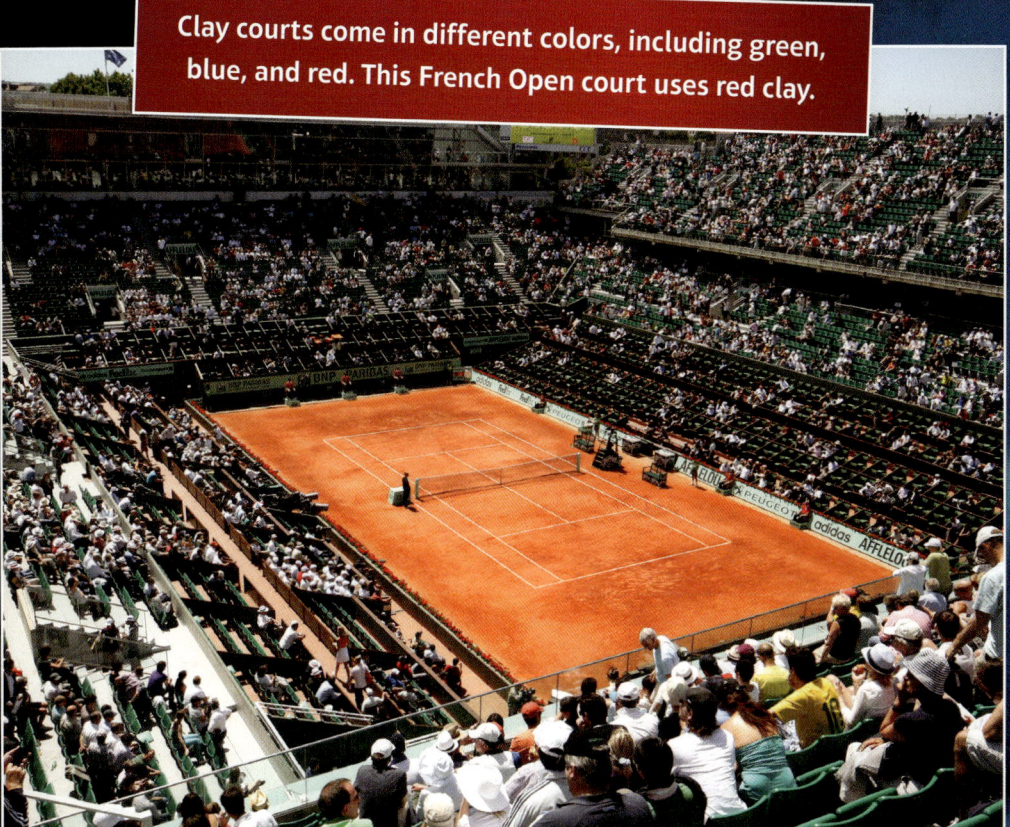

Thousands of men and women play pro tennis. So how do you pick the G.O.A.T.? The sport's long history, its many amazing players, and the variety of tennis events make choosing no easy task. Read on to find out more about some of tennis's best players!

BJÖRN BORG

Growing up in Sweden, Björn Borg loved to play hockey. When summer arrived and the ice melted, he picked up a tennis racket. At first, Björn always gripped the racket with both hands as though it was a hockey stick. As he practiced, he learned that he could hit better forehand shots with just one hand on the racket. But unlike most top players, he used two hands for backhand shots throughout his career.

Borg excelled at tennis and turned pro in 1973 at 17. Soon he reached the top of the pro tennis world. He won the French Open in 1974. At the time, he was the youngest player to ever win the major. He won it again in 1975. Then, beginning in 1978, he won the French Open four times in a row. Borg retired from pro tennis in 1983 at just 26.

BJÖRN BORG STATS

► Borg's career singles record was 606–123.

► In 1976, Borg became the youngest man to win Wimbledon.

► He won the Wimbledon singles title every year from 1976 to 1980.

► Borg won 11 major championships.

► He finished his singles career at the French Open with a 49–2 record.

PETE SAMPRAS

Pete Sampras was born on August 12, 1971, near Washington, DC. In 1978, he moved with his family to California and began playing tennis. At 14, Pete adopted a pro-style, one-handed backhand. He also improved his serve. The changes made Pete one of the hardest-hitting players in tennis. As a pro, his serves regularly topped 130 miles (209 km) per hour.

Sampras won his first major just after his 19th birthday. In the 1990 US Open final, he beat superstar Andre Agassi. Sampras became the youngest man to ever win the US Open. He wasn't at his best on clay courts and never won the French Open. But on grass and hard courts, few players could match his power. Sampras won Wimbledon seven times, the US Open five times, and the Australian Open twice.

PETE SAMPRAS STATS

► Sampras's pro singles record was 762–222.

► He won **14 major singles events**, the fourth most in men's history.

► Sampras was the **top-ranked men's player from 1993 to 1998**.

► He won 64 pro singles events.

► He earned more than $43 million in prize money.

ROD LAVER

Growing up, Rod Laver was short and skinny. He moved so slowly on the court that a fellow player nicknamed him the Rocket as a joke. As a pro, Laver moved more quickly than he had as a young boy. But he was smaller than most of his opponents. Laver won by outworking other players. He played with a quick, fiery style and always kept fighting.

Laver hit his shots with topspin. Hitting the ball a certain way would make it spin forward as it flew. Topspin sent the ball down to the court more quickly. That allowed Laver to hit balls with more power and still keep them inside the court. His spirit and skill helped him win the Grand Slam as an amateur in 1962. Then he won it again in 1969 as a pro. Laver is the only player in tennis history to win two singles Grand Slams.

ROD LAVER STATS

► Laver's pro singles record was **576–146**.

► He won **200 pro and amateur events**.

► Laver was the **top-ranked singles player in the world from 1964–1970**.

► He won 11 major singles titles.

► He was the first pro tennis player to earn $1 million or more in prize money.

CHRIS EVERT

Chris Evert began playing tennis at the age of six. She learned from her father, Jimmy Evert, a pro tennis player and coach. Her father taught some of the world's best players, including three-time major winner Jennifer Capriati. But Chris proved to be his best student. As a teenager, she started beating top-ranked pro players. Other players noticed her calm, confident style. Chris always worked hard and never relaxed during a match.

Evert played her best matches on clay. From August 1973 to May 1979, she won every match she played on clay. The 125-match winning streak is an all-time record for a pro player on a single surface. She also played well at the US Open. She won the event six times and finished second three times. Evert's 101 match victories at the US Open were the most for any player until Serena Williams reached 102 victories in 2020.

CHRIS EVERT STATS

► Evert had a career singles record of 1,304–144.

► She set a record by winning more than 90 percent of her pro matches.

► Evert won 18 major singles events. She is tied with Martina Navratilova for third on the all-time women's list.

► In 1984, she became the first pro player to win 1,000 or more matches.

► From 1972 to 1989, Evert ranked fourth or higher in the world rankings.

#6

NOVAK DJOKOVIC

Growing up in Belgrade, Serbia, Novak Djokovic enjoyed skiing and soccer. But starting at the age of four, tennis was his passion. In elementary school, he started working with tennis coach Jelena Genčić . While his friends goofed around and played games after school, Novak practiced tennis. Neither rain nor snow stopped him from practicing. He practiced tennis even on holidays.

When he was 14, Novak became the European singles and doubles champion for his age group.

Djokovic became a pro player in 2003. His first major win was the 2008 Australian Open. In both 2011 and 2015, he won all the majors except the French Open. Then Djokovic won the 2016 Australian Open and French Open. Though he didn't win the events in the same year, Djokovic became the first player to hold all four majors at once since Rod Laver did in 1969.

NOVAK DJOKOVIC STATS

▶ Djokovic's career singles record is 932–190.

▶ He ranks third in all-time major singles titles with 18.

▶ Djokovic has earned more than $145 million in prize money.

▶ He has won 81 singles events.

▶ Djokovic won a bronze medal at the 2008 Olympic Games in Beijing, China.

#5

MARTINA NAVRATILOVA

Martina Navratilova had one of the longest and most successful careers in tennis history. She started her pro career in 1973 at 16. At 25, she had won just three major singles titles. But by focusing on healthful food and body training, she began to dominate the tennis world.

Navratilova ended her career with 18 major singles titles. She is tied with Chris Evert for third all time. But that's only part of Navratilova's incredible record. She won 31 major doubles titles, the most in tennis history. She also won 10 major mixed doubles titles. Combined, Navratilova holds the all-time record for men's and women's tennis with 59 major championships. Her final title came when she won mixed doubles at the US Open in 2006. Just one month before her 50th birthday, Navratilova became the oldest player to ever win a major.

MARTINA NAVRATILOVA STATS

▶ Navratilova's combined singles and doubles record was 2,189–362.

▶ Her 2,189 wins are an all-time record.

▶ Navratilova won 167 singles titles and 177 doubles titles.

▶ She won Wimbledon a record nine times, including six years in a row.

▶ Navratilova won the Player of the Year award seven times.

STEFFI GRAF

Steffi Graf was born in Mannheim, West Germany, on June 14, 1969. She grew up in a tennis family. Before she was four years old, Steffi received a racket from her parents. She was so small that they had to cut down the racket's handle for her to use it. She began by hitting tennis balls with her father in the family living room. Steffi played her first tournament at the age of five. She won the event a year later.

Graf's pro career began when she was 13. In 1983, she ranked 90th in the world. She reached the top spot in 1987 and didn't rank lower than second for more than 10 years. In 1988, Graf won all four majors to complete the Grand Slam. At the Olympic Games in October, she won the gold medal in women's singles. Her amazing feat was called the Golden Slam.

STEFFI GRAF STATS

- Graf finished her pro singles career with 900 wins and 115 losses.

- She ranks second with **22** major singles titles.

- From 1988 to 1996, Graf won Wimbledon seven times.

- Graf's pro record includes winning streaks of 64, 46, 45, and 44 matches.

- She is the only women's player to win each major event at least four times.

#3

RAFAEL NADAL

Some tennis players like the speed of a hard court. Others feel more comfortable on grass. Rafael Nadal prefers clay. He won the French Open for the first time in 2005, starting a streak of four straight wins there. Beginning in 2010, he won the French Open five times in a row. Then he won it every year from 2017 to 2020. Nadal's 13 French Open wins are the most of any player at a major event.

One reason for Nadal's success is his incredible forehand. On clay, the ball bounces higher and more slowly than on other surfaces. The big, slow bounces allow Nadal to get into position to blast his forehand. But he doesn't need a clay surface to win major events. He won the 2009 Australian Open, two Wimbledon titles, and four US Open championships.

RAFAEL NADAL STATS

► Nadal's career singles record is 1,002–202.

► With 20 major singles titles, Nadal is tied with Roger Federer for first on the men's career list.

► He plays left-handed and often uses a two-handed backhand.

► Nadal has won 86 pro singles events.

► The 2020 championship match was Nadal's 100th win at the French Open.

ROGER FEDERER

Growing up in Basel, Switzerland, Roger Federer loved sports. When he was 12, he decided to focus on tennis. He spent about 10 hours each week practicing tennis and training his body. In 1988, Federer played his first pro tennis match. He was 17. In 2003, he won Wimbledon and became the first man from Switzerland to win a major title.

The Wimbledon victory was the first of five straight titles Federer won at the event. He fell to Rafael Nadal in the 2008 final. But Federer roared back in 2009 to win Wimbledon for the sixth time in seven years. He has been to 31 major finals in his career, winning 20 of them. Of his 11 finals losses, 10 were to Nadal or Djokovic.

ROGER FEDERER STATS

▶ Federer is tied with Rafael Nadal for first on the all-time men's list with 20 major singles wins.

▶ Federer has won 1,242 career singles matches and lost just 271.

▶ He has spent 310 weeks ranked number one in the world. That's more than any other men's player.

▶ At 36, Federer became the oldest men's player to ever rank number one in the world.

▶ He has won 103 pro singles events.

#1

SERENA WILLIAMS

At the age of five, Serena Williams was already on track to become a tennis superstar. With their father as coach, Serena and her sister Venus practiced for hours every day. As pro players, the Williams sisters teamed up to rule doubles. In 1999, they won doubles titles at the French Open and the US Open. The next year, they won the Olympic gold medal in doubles. In total, the Williams sisters

Serena Williams (*left*) and Venus Williams (*right*)

have won three Olympic doubles golds and 14 major doubles titles.

Serena Williams's record in singles is even better. She won her first singles major at the 1999 US Open. In 2002–2003, she achieved the Serena Slam by holding all four major titles at once. She did it again in 2014–2015. Her 23 major singles championships are more than any other modern player has. Williams's amazing success in the world's most important tennis events makes her the greatest of all time.

SERENA WILLIAMS STATS

▶ Williams's combined singles and doubles record is 1,033–181.

▶ She won the singles gold medal at the 2012 Olympic Games.

▶ Williams has won 73 singles events and 23 doubles events.

▶ She has earned more than $93 million in prize money.

▶ At 35, Williams became the oldest woman to rank number one in the world.

YOUR
G.O.A.T.

IT'S YOUR TURN TO MAKE YOUR OWN G.O.A.T. LIST! Think about the tennis players in this book. They got to the top in their own ways. Some used big, powerful shots to win. Others played with amazing energy, chasing down every ball and never giving up. Reorder the players or list others to create a top-10 list based on your opinions.

Many great players who have won majors and set amazing records aren't included in this book. Explore the Learn More section on page 31 to find out about some of them. Check out books from your library about tennis players and events. Look online for more information, and talk to your friends who like tennis. Who do they think the G.O.A.T. players are? Which players will you add to your top-10 list? It's all up to you!

TENNIS FACTS

▶ The longest pro tennis match took place at Wimbledon in 2010. John Isner beat Nicolas Mahut in a match that lasted 11 hours and five minutes over three days.

▶ In 1988, Steffi Graf won the shortest women's singles match. She crushed Natalya Zvereva in the French Open final in just 32 minutes. Zvereva scored only 13 points against Graf.

▶ Tennis balls used to be white. To make them easier to see on TV, most pro tennis events switched to yellow balls in the 1970s. But Wimbledon used white balls until 1986.

▶ Martina Hingis won the 1997 Australian Open when she was 16. That made her the second-youngest person to win a major. At 15, Lottie Dod won Wimbledon in 1887.

GLOSSARY

amateur: playing a sport without being paid

backhand: a tennis stroke made with the back of the hand turned in the direction in which the hand is moving

doubles: a tennis match with two players on each side

final: the championship match of a tournament

forehand: a tennis stroke made with the palm of the hand turned in the direction in which the hand is moving

Grand Slam: winning all four majors in one year

hard court: a type of tennis court that is usually concrete or asphalt

major: the Australian Open, the French Open, the US Open, or Wimbledon

mixed doubles: a tennis match with one man and one woman on each side

pro: being paid to play a sport

serve: to hit the ball to begin play

singles: tennis matches with one player on each side

topspin: a ball's motion that causes it to rotate forward in the direction it is traveling

LEARN MORE

Ahrens, Niki. *Serena Williams: Tennis Superstar*. Minneapolis: Lerner Publications, 2022.

Derr, Aaron. *Individual Sports of the Summer Games*. Egremont, MA: Red Chair, 2020.

International Tennis Hall of Fame
https://www.tennisfame.com

London, Martha. *Legends of Women's Tennis*. Burnsville, MN: Press Box Books, 2021.

10 Fun Facts about Wimbledon
https://www.sikids.com/the-arena/10-fun-facts-about-wimbledon

Tennis Facts for Kids
https://kids.kiddle.co/Tennis

INDEX

PHOTO ACKNOWLEDGMENTS

Image credits: AP Photo, pp. 4, 9 (bottom), 15 (bottom); AP Photo/Uncredited, pp. 6, 14; Olga Besnard/Shutterstock.com, pp. 7, 23 (bottom); AP Photo/ Anonymous, pp. 8, 12; AP Photo/Bob Dear, p. 9 (top); AP Photo/NewsBase, p. 10; AP Photo/Mark Lennihan, p. 11 (top); AP Photo/Dave Caulkin, p. 11 (bottom); AP Photo/John Rider-Rider, p. 13 (top); AP Photo/Bodini, p. 13 (bottom); AP Photo/Al Messerschmidt Archive, p. 15 (top); AP Photo/Mark Baker, pp. 16, 17 (bottom); AP Photo/Elise Amendola, pp. 17 (top), 27 (top); AP Photo/Laurent Rebours, p. 18; AP Photo/Gill Allen, pp. 19 (top), 21 (bottom); AP Photo/Alastair Grant, p. 19 (bottom); AP Photo/Peter Morgan, p. 20; AP Photo/Lionel Cironneau, p. 21 (top); Leonard Zhukovsky/Shutterstock.com, pp. 22, 26, 27 (bottom); AP Photo/Christophe Saidi/ SIPA, p. 23 (top); AP Photo/Anja Niedringhaus, pp. 24, 25 (top); Anthony Correia/ Shutterstock.com, p. 25 (bottom); irin-k/Shutterstock.com, p. 28.

Cover: Adam Vilimek/Shutterstock.com (tennis court); Leonard Zhukovsky/ Shutterstock.com (Roger Federer and Serena Williams).